the boy who wouldn't go to bed

For
Caledonia

With thanks to
Ian Butterworth,
Annie Eaton,
and Ted Dewan

First published in the United States 1997
by Dial Books for Young Readers
A Member of Penguin Putnam Inc.
375 Hudson Street
New York, New York 10014

Published in Great Britain 1996
by Transworld Publishers
Printed in Belgium
First Edition
3 5 7 9 10 8 6 4 2

Library of Congress Cataloging in Publication Data
Cooper, Helen (Helen F.)
The boy who wouldn't go to bed/Helen Cooper.
p.   cm.
Summary: A boy who does not want to go to bed has a
series of imaginary encounters with a tiger, soldiers, the moon,
and others, all of whom convince him to change his mind.
ISBN 0-8037-2253-2
[1. Bedtime—Fiction. 2. Sleep—Fiction.
3. Imagination—Fiction.] I. Title.
PZ7.C7855Bo 1997 [E]—dc21 96-44425 CIP AC

The artwork for this book was prepared with watercolor paints.

the boy who wouldn't go to bed

Helen Cooper

Dial Books for Young Readers New York

"Bedtime!"
said the mother.

"No!"
said the boy,
playing in his car.
"It's still light."

"Because it's summer,"
said the mother.

A little while later . . .

"Bedtime!"
said the mother.

"NO!"
said the boy,
playing in his car.
"I'm going to stay up
all night."

"Oh, no you're not!"
said the mother.

But the boy revved up his car …
vrrrooom-chugga-chug …
then drove away
as fast as he could,
and the mother couldn't
catch him.

He hadn't driven very far at all
before he met a tiger.
"Let's play at roaring,"
said the boy.

But the tiger was too tired.
"Nighttime is for snoring,
not roaring,"
yawned the tiger.
"Come back in the morning.
I'll play with you then."

So off zoomed the boy ...
vrrrooom-chugga-chug ...
till he met a troop
of soldiers.

"Let's have a parade,"
said the boy.
But the soldiers
were too sleepy.

"Nighttime is for
dreaming, not
parading," said the
captain.
"We're going back to
our castle. And so
should you."

Sleepytown
Awakeville
Castle

But the boy
didn't want to. He
trundled away in
his car...
vrrrooom-
chugga-chug...
as fast as he
could.

He stopped for a moment
as a train rolled by.
"Race you to the station," called the boy.

But the train was too tired.

"Nighttime is for resting, not racing," said the train.

"I'm going home to my depot, and so should you."

But still the boy rumbled along the
road … vrrrooom-chugga-chug … till he
met some musicians.

"Let's have a party and dance all
night," said the boy.

But the musicians were too drowsy.
"We're really awfully tired," they said.
"Give us a ride home, and we'll
play you a lullaby instead."

The musicians played
such a sweet tune
that the sun was lulled
to sleep and the
moon came out.

The boy's car went slower...

and slower...

and slower...

and soon the musicians
were sound asleep.

Then the boy's
car stopped....
It had fallen
asleep too.

The boy looked up at
the moon.
"Can't we have a midnight
feast?" he wailed.

"It's bedtime,"
sighed the moon drowsily.
And even the moon closed
her eyes and dozed off.

Now the boy had to
push the car
in the dusky dark.

It was hard work.

And soon he'd gone as far as he could.
He stood quite still, awake and alone,
with the sleeping world around him.

But there was someone else who was not asleep.

Someone who was looking for the boy …

and getting nearer...

and nearer...

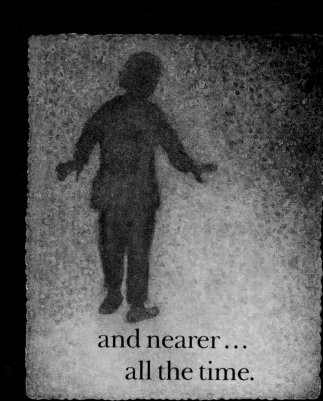

and nearer...
all the time.

Someone who was ever so sleepy,
but couldn't go to bed until the boy did.

It was the mother.

And the boy hugged her.

Then the mother lifted up the boy with one
arm, and pushed the car with the other....
(She was a very strong mother.)

And she trundled and bundled them
all the way home.

"Bedtime?"
asked the boy sleepily.
"No," whispered the mother.
"You said you were
staying up
all night!"

"Y-a-w-n,"
said the boy.

"All right then,"
said the mother.

"Good night."